ACKNOWLEDGMENTS

Special thanks is owed to the
following individuals for their help.

Carol Rosegg—Assistant Photographer

Andrea Green	Estelle Rothstein
Anita Gold	Joe Danisi
Diana Argiros	Paul Lieberman
Karen Ambrogio	Howard Elias
Merril Abramson	Gerry Green
Joanne Fuchs	Ace Hardware
Laura Bohnenberger	F&D Luncheonette
Steve Ehrhardt	Doug Shavel
Charles Rosenblum	Mr. J. Hershkowitz
Rosalie Green	Naomi Wolfe

For Rich

Toni's Crowd

TONI'S CROWD

BY ELLEN RABINOWICH
PHOTOGRAPHS BY
G. RICHARDSON COOK

A TRIUMPH BOOK

FRANKLIN WATTS
NEW YORK | LONDON | 1978

Library of Congress Cataloging in Publication Data

Rabinowich, Ellen.
    Toni's crowd.

    (A Triumph book)
    SUMMARY: Sandi's attempt to become one of
the crowd in her new ninth grade is complicated by
her parents' insistence that she befriend the un-
popular daughter of her father's new boss.
    [1. Friendship—Fiction]   I. Title.
PZ7.R109To   [Fic]   78–1549
ISBN 0-531-02210-2

R.L. 2.5 Spache Revised Formula

Toni's Crowd

Mom's voice went off like an alarm clock. I buried my head under the pillow.

"Wake up Sandi! Time for school! You need time for breakfast."

For Mom, eating breakfast should have been one of the Ten Commandments. Thou Shalt Eat Breakfast.

I didn't mind school. What I minded was being new. In the ninth grade. In the middle of the term. When friendships were already made. And as hard to break into as the Federal Reserve. That I minded. Plenty.

"Don't forget your books."

I don't know how Mom thinks school can help an idiot like me.

New Jersey's Parkside High was just like my old school in Wisconsin. It had small classrooms, dusty blackboards, and big clocks that helped mark time like a calendar. What it didn't have was a place for me.

I stood alone in the schoolyard. The kids stood in clusters. Each cluster was like a state on the map. After two weeks, I knew which state I wanted to move to. It was populated by five girls. Toni. Marlene. Susan. Ann. And Kathy.

Toni's crowd.

Why them? Because they didn't act dumb. They said funny things. And older boys talked to them. I knew they were my crowd. Deep down. Where you know certain things.

But they didn't know. They were cool. They didn't recognize anyone else.

"Today, class," Mr. Turner said, "let's talk about books for outside reading." I loved English. But Mr. Turner didn't. He made everything sound so boring. Only his high squeaky voice kept most of the class awake.

"Any suggestions?"

I raised my hand.

"Yes, Sandi."

"What about *Tough Chick*," I said. "It's all about gangs in the big city."

The whole class laughed.

Mr. Turner didn't. He cleared his throat instead.

"If you want sex and violence, watch television," he squeaked.

Typical.

After class Kathy came up to me. "That was pretty neat," she smiled. "Telling old Squeaky about that trash."

My heart changed places with my stomach. Kathy talked to me! And, I think she was paying me a compliment!

"I read it too," she said. Her smile was as friendly as United. "But I hide it from my parents."

"Me too," I grinned.

Kathy walked down the hall with me. As we talked about our private trash collections, Toni passed. She arched her eyebrows at Kathy. Toni had great eyebrows for arching. They were jet black. Like her short curly hair. "Who's your new friend?" she asked.

Kathy introduced us. My fingers made damp streaks across my books. Toni was the leader of Kathy's crowd. And she wasn't thrilled to meet me.

Toni grabbed Kathy's arm. "I have something to

tell you," she said. She whispered into Kathy's ear. They burst out laughing. "Come on," Toni tugged Kathy's arm again. "I'll tell you all about it."

Kathy waved goodbye, and they walked off whispering and laughing. My heart felt like a big lump of clay. Winning Toni over wasn't going to be easy.

After school, I went to the drugstore. I looked for lipstick, eye shadow, and rouge. Kathy and Toni wore makeup. So did the other girls. But I didn't know which colors to choose. Goodbye, two week's allowance. I bought a couple of each.

Later, I tried on the different shades in my room. Finally, I arrived at something that looked pretty natural. However, my parents had a different opinion.

"What's that junk all over your face?" my father asked as I sat down to dinner.

"Revlon's Apricot Glow."

"Well wash it off," Dad glowered. "It looks awful."

"But Dad. All the girls in school wear makeup."

Mom's anger always built slowly. Like a summer storm. But Dad's came fast. Like a hurricane. Between the two of them they had all the crummy weather conditions covered. "Well you're not," Dad yelled. "Maybe lipstick. But that's all."

I looked to Mom for support, but she just upheld the decree.

"Your father's right," she nodded.

It always amazed me. Mom and Dad fought like cats and dogs. But when it came to me, they were like turtledoves. United by a common enemy.

The next day I went back to the drugstore. I bought a small mirror, a jar of cold cream, and a pack of Kleenex. No makeup, huh? I'd wipe it off while I rode home on the school bus.

During the next few days, Kathy started talking to me. In class, after class. Toni didn't like that. At all. Whenever she saw us together, she called Kathy away.

But Kathy liked me. Whenever she saw me she flashed her big cover girl smile. (Kathy must have brushed with bleach. She had the whitest teeth.)

One morning, she asked me to join them.

"Meet us in the girl's room. On the second floor. At one forty-five sharp," she said.

"But I'll be in Math class."

Kathy tossed back her straight blonde hair. "We'll all be in class, silly. Get a hall pass."

Getting a pass from Ms. Terry's class wasn't easy. Someone already had it. One of the Board of Education's Ten Commandments: Thou Shalt Not Allow Two People on a Pass. Where there's a will, there's a way. Mom's phrase finally paid off. I opened my ballpoint and smeared ink on my hands. I got a pass.

I walked into the girls' room. Toni and Susan sat on the window ledge. Marlene and Ann stood in front of the mirror. Where was Kathy?

"I have to look gorgeous for eighth period," Marlene was saying, running a comb through strawberry blonde bangs.

Marlene might have wanted to look gorgeous, but Ann already was. She had almond-shaped eyes, a tiny nose, and a small clef in her chin. She also had beautiful wavy, dark hair.

Suddenly, I hated my straight hair. I knew "natural" was in. But why couldn't mine be naturally beautiful like Ann's.

"Hi everybody!" Thank god, it was Kathy. I was beginning to feel invisible.

Kathy introduced me to her friends. Of course, I knew who *they* were.

Everyone smiled and said hello. Except Toni. She stared at my inky hands.

"I thought finger painting went out with the second grade," she laughed.

Marlene and Susan giggled. Then they grew quiet. Waiting for a comeback.

Sometimes, I can think fast. But with everyone waiting, my mind was like a car without gas.

"Maybe she was running her fingers through Johnny Wimple's hair," Marlene suggested.

Everyone howled. Johnny Wimple was the school greaser. His oily black hair looked like it hadn't been washed in years.

Again, I tried to think of some clever retort, but Toni beat me to it. "Are you kidding?" she laughed. "She'd never get her fingers out."

While everyone giggled, Toni drew a cigarette from her purse.

"Toni," Susan warned. "Your lungs are going to turn to soot." Kathy told me that Susan was a health food freak. She was also one of the best athletes in gym. Even though she was a little plump.

Toni stared down at her flat chest. "What lungs?" she laughed. Gee, I thought enviously, Toni has an answer for everything.

But Toni didn't light up. Instead she went into a deep slouch, stuffed her hands in her pockets, and dangled the cigarette between her lips. "Anyone seen my smokes?" she asked from the side of her mouth.

Everyone laughed. She was doing Johnny Wimple.

Suddenly, I heard myself squeaking. Just like Mr. Turner. "Your cigarettes," I squeaked. "Why Simple Wimple, you ate the pack last week."

Everyone laughed. At last. I said something right.

Then Susan and Ann joined in. Susan played our gym teacher. Toni pretended she wouldn't play ball. Ann was a student with a dirty uniform. Soon, we were all doubled over from laughing. They were great mimics.

Only on the way out did I stop giggling. Everyone promised to telephone each other. Except for me. I was left out. Back to being an unlisted number.

When I got home, Mom was waiting.

"Your room's a disgrace," was the general meaning of her ten-minute tirade.

After I went to my room, Mom called. She'll do anything to avoid speaking in a normal tone.

"Sandi. I want you to wear a dress tonight. And do something with your hair."

"Why?" I asked. Mom hated the way my hair fell in my eyes. But why tonight? Was it company time?

"We're going to dinner at the Frampton's."

The Framptons. Christ. Martha Frampton sat next to me in Science. She looked like something out of a test tube. Pale eyes, pale skin, pale hair. Colorless. And personality count: zero. The only reason I

remembered her was that when she borrowed a pencil, she made such a big deal of returning it.

One of Sandi Peter's Ten Commandments: Thou Shalt Not Team Up with a Loser. I learned that one in camp. After I made friends with creepy Joan Harris, I was branded. None of the popular girls would talk to me.

I walked to the top of the stairs. "Mom," I said. "Maybe I'll stay home. I'm not feeling so hot."

"Well." My mother corrected in an irritated tone. She rested her hand on her hip. "The Framptons are very important to your father's career. And they have a daughter just your age. It won't kill you to come."

Maybe it will, I thought as I threw on my putrid purple that Mom loved so much. Maybe I'll choke during dinner. Then they'll be sorry.

You couldn't exactly call the Frampton place a house. It was a residence. In other words, a mansion. At least I can't accuse Martha of being stuck up, I thought as the maid answered the door. Her nose was always pointed toward the floor.

"So glad you could come," Mr. and Mrs. Frampton greeted us.

Martha barely managed a smile. I could tell this evening was going to be really exciting.

"What a marvelous piece," Mom cooed over an overstuffed chair. I locked into the chandeliers. Now they were something. Like waterfalls of diamonds.

Since my parents really outdid themselves admiring all their junk, Mr. Frampton invited them on a grand tour of the house. Leaving Martha and me to break the ice.

At first neither of us spoke. My parents made me come, I thought. But they can't make me talk.

"We're in the same Science class," Martha finally said.

Oh yes. We were off to a zippy start. "Yeah."

But during dinner I began feeling sorry for Martha. Her parents bragged about her like she was some kind of prize. But they never let her talk. Every time she tried to say something, they cut her off. I could tell Martha was really embarrassed. Her pale skin grew lighter and lighter.

"May I be excused?" Martha asked during coffee and liqueurs.

Mrs. Frampton looked surprised, but my parents nearly fell off their chairs. They'd been trying to get me to talk politely for years.

"Why don't you show Sandi your room," Mrs. Frampton suggested.

Martha nodded her head while I eyed the brandy. A dinner like that could drive you to drink.

Martha's room had all that money could buy, including a huge four-poster bed with a white lace canopy. I'd always wanted one. A canopy, that is. Dust collectors, Mom called them. But from the way Martha moped around you could tell even *that* didn't make her happy.

I was wondering what we were going to do when Martha shut the door and turned toward me. Was I surprised. Tears filled her light blue eyes.

"I know you're having a terrible time," she said. "But this wasn't my idea. I didn't ask them to invite you."

If it weren't for those eyes, I would have gotten mad. "I'm not having a terrible time," I insisted. I tried to change the subject. "I think your house is really neat. It's so big. Do you have any brothers or sisters?"

Now a tear rolled down Martha's cheek. Christ, I couldn't say anything right. "I had an older brother. He was wounded in Vietnam. He died last year."

I tried to think of something wise and comforting to say. But no one ever died in my family. I reached out and took Martha's hand. "I'm sorry," I said. "I guess you miss him a lot."

Martha sniffed and looked down. "My parents always brag about me," she said softly. "Because I'm all they have left."

I almost felt like crying. How depressing. But parents. That was a subject I could sink my teeth into.

"Your parents," I smiled. "You should hear mine. They're like a vaudeville team. Always bickering and fighting."

Martha laughed. "And mine are high comedy."

Soon Martha and I weren't having such a bad time. Since Mrs. Frampton had carried on about Martha's artwork, I asked to see her drawings.

"They're really not much," Martha said, pulling out big pads.

But they were. She drew mostly pastoral scenes. Lots of cows and chickens. But Martha made them look different than the barnyards of Wisconsin. She drew the animals in a playful comic way. It made me look at them differently.

"That wasn't so bad," Mom said, riding home.

Actually it wasn't. Martha wasn't exciting like Toni's crowd, but she was nice.

"It was alright." I didn't want Mom to think we were the best of friends. She'd be inviting her home for dinner every night.

4

During lunch the next day I sat in my usual place. Alone, by the window. Toni's crowd always sat at a special table. But no one had asked me to join them yet. I'd just have to wait.

"Hi Sandi, anyone sitting here?"

I looked up. It was Martha.

I said no, but I almost felt like saying yes. Toni's crowd didn't know that Martha was okay. If they saw us together, it would be the same story as camp. Branded.

Martha started talking. I tried to concentrate, but it was hard. Toni's crowd were filing out from the cafeteria line. And they had to pass us to get to their table.

Maybe they won't see me, I hoped. I stared at my plate and pretended to be fascinated by my carrots and peas.

Then I heard a voice. Kathy's.

"Hi, Sandi. Why don't you come sit with us."

Suddenly, I hated Martha. I wanted to go. But if I left, I'd hurt her feelings.

"Go ahead, Sandi," Martha said. She picked up her tray, although some food was left. "I have to go to my locker."

Before I could answer, Martha was off.

"What a zero," Kathy said. "Are you two friends?"

"No," I quickly said. After that verdict, how could I say yes. "But she's not so bad," I added. I did feel bad about her leaving.

Kathy looked uncertain. "Really? Well I don't think Toni likes her very much."

I wanted to ask why, but I didn't get a chance. When we were almost at Toni's table, the fire drill rang.

"Listen," Kathy whispered before we parted. "Everybody's going over Toni's after school. Want to come?"

Did I? Is the Pope Catholic? I nodded yes.

Toni's house was middle class like mine, but a little bigger. Certainly no mansion. It didn't have to be. It was Toni's.

Susan answered the doorbell. "We're upstairs," she smiled. "Come on up."

Stuffed animals filled Toni's room. They were everywhere. On the bed. Tables. Chairs. Toni lounged on the bed, polishing her fingernails. Ann sat on the floor, between an elephant and a tiger. With her flowing hair and almond-shaped eyes, she fit right in. A beautiful jungle queen.

I didn't know where to sit. I was afraid of upsetting the menagerie.

"Pull up a piece of floor," Toni said.

I sat next to a duck. The duck had more room than I. It didn't matter. I felt special just being there. Like I was part of Toni's inner circle.

We didn't have much time to chat. Soon, Kathy and Marlene came in.

"You got it?" Toni asked Kathy.

Kathy produced an album from a brown paper wrapper. "For your special listening enjoyment," she crooned like a radio disc jockey. "The Silver Convention."

"Super!" Ann cried.

"Let's give a listen," Toni yelled, scrambling off her bed to grab the album. "Come on."

Soon, disco music shook Toni's basement walls. Toni grabbed Kathy. Marlene grabbed Susan. They twirled and turned into the Hustle, the latest disco dance.

Ann extended her hand. "Come on," she said.

I looked down. I was a good dancer. But they weren't doing the Hustle in Wisconsin. "I don't know how," I blushed.

Ann's almond-shaped eyes widened into chestnuts. "You don't!" Then she smiled. "It's simple. I'll show you."

At first, I felt like a total clod. I was used to dancing by myself. But Ann was a great teacher. She might have looked like a delicate princess, but she was far from helpless. She twirled me with such force, it was almost impossible to trip up. Soon, I didn't even have to count. I let the music flow through me, and twirled around like a disco queen.

"You're a fast learner," Ann smiled. "It took me weeks to count to six."

"Thanks," I beamed. Now my heart danced with my feet.

Only when we changed partners did I lose step. I was with Kathy. And, Toni was staring at us.

"Kathy," she said finally. "You're joggling."

At first I thought she was criticizing our dancing.

"You would too," Kathy laughed, "if you took off that silly harness."

Toni twirled, but didn't answer. "Okay have it your way," she finally laughed. "But don't come crying to me when the guys get you behind the A & P."

Kathy let go of my arms so I almost spun across the floor. "That's ridiculous," she said. "You sound like my great-grandmother."

"That's right," Ann piped in. "Not wearing a bra doesn't make you a tramp. Just liberated."

This time Toni lost a beat. "Well, if you want your clothes to hang funny that's your business." She tried a fancy twirl, but didn't quite make it.

The music stopped. Was I glad. By this time I was stumbling all over my feet. Besides, dancing was fun, but this was important.

"It's bras that give you an unnatural shape," Ann insisted.

Now Susan, the sports fiend, joined in. "I agree, but you should wear them for support in gym."

Toni laughed. "We're talking about bras. Not jockstraps."

When it came down to it, only Marlene agreed with Toni. I noticed she did that a lot.

"I think they make clothes look better," she said. Then she turned to me. "You wear one, don't you? What do you think?"

Me? I thought the whole thing was fascinating. I remembered how I begged Mom for a bra. Now a lot of women were taking them off. "Well," I said. "I guess it depends on how big you are and what you're wearing."

Kathy, Ann, and Susan took that as a vote for their side. "See," Ann said to Toni. "You're outnumbered."

For a moment, Toni looked really flustered. Then she told us she had an idea. She called it a brainstorm. I called it brain damage. It was so awful.

"Okay," she smirked. "Let's see how liberated you really are. I'll throw a party this Saturday night. And you can all invite your own dates."

First there was dead silence. Then Kathy spoke. "That's fine by me," she said.

"Me, too," said Ann.

But Susan groaned. "That's easy for you," she said. "You have boyfriends."

"But this is your big chance," Toni told her. "You can invite Tommy McAllister."

Everyone laughed. I guessed Susan was crazy about him.

"Very funny," said Susan.

Toni batted her eyelashes. "I'm not afraid to invite who I like. Even though I wear a bra." She turned to me. "Are you?"

Me? I didn't even know who I liked. But I was lucky to be invited at all. "Of course not," I said.

"Good. Then it's settled," Toni said. "And everybody better work fast. The party is this Saturday night."

Who could I ask? I knew who it couldn't be. It couldn't be someone they liked. It couldn't be someone they considered a creep. And it couldn't be anyone that would turn me down. All those "couldn't be's" narrowed my choices.

Then I had a brainstorm. A real one. I'd ask Scott Miles. He was a year older, nice looking, and funny. He always kidded around with me when I went into his uncle's hardware store. Which I did a lot. Ever since we moved, Mom kept sending me for stuff to fix the house.

But the brainstorm part was this: Scott didn't go to my school. He lived in the next town. He just worked for his uncle after school. If he said no, I'd never have to see him again. I'd just buy my hardware somewhere else.

After school the next day I ran home and changed my clothes. Again and again. Nothing seemed right. Finally I found something I liked. I combed my hair a half dozen times. Mom wasn't

home so I put on some makeup. I tried to think what to say. My mind went blank. You'll think on the way, I told myself.

Outside the store I put on more lipstick. The first coat was bitten off. I practiced. "Would you like to come to a party?" No. Too forward. "What are you doing Saturday night?" No. Too risky. Then I got it. I went inside.

"Hi, Scott," I said.

"Hi," Scott smiled. "How's school?"

"Oh fine." I answered as if my mind was on something else. I walked around the store. I pretended to look very hard. I began to hum.

The third time I passed Scott he stopped me. "Maybe I can help you find it," he smiled.

"Maybe you can. Where are the corkscrews?"

Scott showed me. Of course, I knew all along.

"Your Mom giving a party?" he asked.

"No. One of my friends."

Scott gave a low whistle. "And you're serving wine?" He seemed interested.

I laughed. "Maybe. Maybe not. It never hurts to be prepared."

Scott's eyes lit up. "Sounds like an OK party."

Everything had gone according to plan. Now was the hard part. I sucked in my breath. "It might be. Want to come?"

"With you?" he asked.

I didn't trust my voice. I nodded.

"Sure," he smiled. "Why not?"

Suddenly, I grew very nervous. I could hardly give Toni's address. It was okay. Scott had delivered some things to her house.

That night I could hardly fall asleep. I was going to a party! With my new friends! And Scott was coming with me! I never felt so happy.

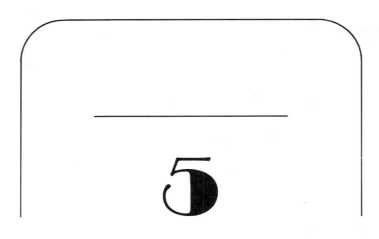

5

"Who wants to shop for party decorations with me?" Toni asked the next day.

Kathy had a dentist appointment. Susan had volleyball practice. Ann had to take care of her little brother. That left Marlene and me.

"I'll come," I volunteered.

I could tell Toni wasn't too thrilled by my offer. I know she would have preferred Kathy. Actually I wasn't too thrilled either. Toni had such a quick tongue. I still didn't feel very comfortable with her.

Maybe it will be easier to get Toni to like me without everyone else around, I thought as I walked toward Woolworth's Five-and-Ten. People are often different when they're alone.

But when I got to Woolworth's, Toni wasn't outside. I found her inside. With Marlene, by the party supplies.

"This stuff is so babyish," Toni frowned, after we'd said hello. "I want this party to be really different. Anybody got any ideas?"

My mind worked overtime. No help.

"I know," Toni smiled, picking up some silver streamers. "I'll decorate in silver and black. It'll be ultra chic." She looked at us. "What do you think?"

Marlene and I agreed. Why hadn't I thought of that?

Soon we were having a great time scouring the store. Searching for stuff to fit into Toni's color scheme. Toni found some black balloons. Marlene dug up silver tinsel left over from Christmas. And finally, I found something.

"How about this?" I held up a bottle of nail-polish. Silver glitter. "We can paint kids' names on the balloons."

Toni eagerly nodded her head. "Great idea!"

Marlene frowned. She wished she had thought of that.

"But maybe I'll paint faces instead," Toni laughed.

Soon we had everything. But as we passed the cosmetics, Toni stopped.

"This lipstick is super," she said, twisting the bottom so a bronze color poked out. "But the price. Outrageous!"

I stared. With a flick of Toni's wrist, the small tube disappeared into her purse.

Toni smiled. So did Marlene. I was dumbfounded. Shoplifting?

"Ever boost before?" Toni asked me.

I shook my head no. I guessed that boost meant stealing.

"Well try it. It's easy."

I really didn't want to. "Suppose we get caught?" I asked.

Toni stared at me like my brains were made of marshmallow. "What's the matter? Afraid?"

"No," I lied. "It's just that . . ."

"Well go ahead then," Toni laughed. "Try it."

Somehow I knew I had to. If I didn't, Toni would never be my friend.

I looked around for something to take. I stared at bins of lipsticks, rouges, and powder. Suddenly, it all looked the same. I didn't want anything.

"What about this notepaper," Toni pointed to a shelf across the aisle. "It's so corny."

I looked. Gold stripes bordered the edges. But corny? I couldn't tell. I was too nervous.

"All right." I looked around. No one was watching. I picked the notepaper off the shelf.

"Can I help you?"

I whirled around in terror. Caught, I thought. Caught red-handed. Only my hands were white. From fear.

A saleswoman stood behind me. She was pretty mean looking. "Can I help you?" she repeated. Then she smiled. Of course. The notepaper was only in my hand.

I wanted to answer yes. Help me out of here.

I didn't answer. Toni did. "Where are the can openers?" Her voice was smooth as butter. "I can't find them anywhere."

Now the coast was clear. Just like in a gangster movie, Toni lured the guard away.

I barely bothered to look this time. I grabbed the notepaper and stashed it deep in my purse.

There. Done. I felt hot and cold at once.

"Let's go," I urged Marlene.

Marlene gave me one of Toni's marshmallow brain stares. "No. We have to wait for Toni."

Wait? With stolen property burning a hole in my purse. Suddenly I understood the meaning of hot.

"I'll meet you outside," I said.

Marlene shrugged. "Do what you like."

I walked toward the door trying to act naturally. My footsteps seemed to echo through the store. Any moment I expected to be stopped.

Don't be silly, I told myself. No one saw. I walked out the exit door. Like any ordinary solid citizen.

Once outside, I ran across the street. Now that I was safe, I felt kind of giddy. I had the notepaper. And, no one had caught me.

Toni and Marlene didn't come out right away. Five minutes passed. Ten minutes. Were they caught, I wondered. If they were, would they rat on me? Damn, I was thinking like a criminal already.

Finally Toni and Marlene came out. They looked pleased. I breathed a sigh of relief.

Toni pointed to a hidden driveway. "Come on. I'll show you what I got."

Toni opened her purse. It was like watching a magician. She pulled out ribbons, a miniature picture frame, and a few other things.

Marlene gave a good follow-up performance. Her purse was loaded too.

I felt like a loser with just my notepaper.

"Let's see the paper," Toni said. "Maybe we'll trade."

I reached deep into my purse. I couldn't understand it. Something cold mushed against my hand.

The cold cream! That I used on the bus! The top must have come off.

I pulled the notepaper out. Cold cream coated the plastic wrapping. Little bits of candy wrappers stuck to the edges.

"What in the world . . ." Toni said.

I didn't want to look like a total loser. "Oh," I said casually. "I stole some cold cream. The top must have fallen off."

Marlene and Toni laughed. "Good girl," Toni patted me on the back. "You're learning."

Soon, we split up to go home. "Oh I almost forgot," Toni yelled. "I changed the time of the party. It's eight o'clock now."

On the way home I decided to stop by the hardware store. I had to tell Scott about the new time. Also, I was feeling kind of high. I wasn't crazy about stealing. But I had done it. And, Toni and Marlene seemed proud of me. Somehow, I felt like nothing could hurt me now.

But outside the hardware store I lost my nerve. What if Scott had changed his mind?

I went through my lipstick routine again. I combed my hair. Be brave, I told myself as I walked in.

At first I didn't see Scott. Then I looked up. He was high on a ladder. Fixing a shelf.

"Hallo up there," I called, imitating a sailor. I *was* feeling good.

Scott looked down and smiled. But the ladder jiggled a bit. "There still a party?" he asked.

My heart did a little jig. *He* was worried.

"Sure there's a party," I answered. "I just figured you might not want to be an hour early."

"Good figuring," Scott smiled as he climbed down. "How many bells?"

Bells? I knew that sailors used bells to announce time. But how many? "When the clock strikes eight," I said.

Scott laughed. Then his uncle walked in.

"Want to get a soda?" Scott asked, after he introduced us.

"Sure."

I'd never seen Scott outside the store. He really looked different. Much better, actually. The sunlight gave a golden tint to his dirty blonde hair. And I thought his eyes were brown. But they were green, now. A little chill ran up my spine. Scott was pretty good-looking.

"Hey, you're staring," Scott said.

"No I'm not," I blushed.

Scott put his arm around me. Playfully. The chill changed into a funny tingle.

"That's okay," Scott teased. "Most women can't take their eyes off me."

"Maybe that's because you're so funny looking," I teased back.

Scott didn't have much time. His uncle expected him back in the store. But in those few minutes I found out something really exciting.

"Does your uncle pay you?" I asked, after we'd ordered cherry cokes.

Scott laughed. "You bet. I need that money."

"You do? Why?" I almost bit my tongue. What if Scott was poverty-stricken.

But Scott just laughed again. Then he lowered his voice. "To pay my debts. I'm in up to my neck."

"No, come on. Tell me." I knew he was teasing.

"Well . . ." Scott suddenly looked shy. "I take acting lessons."

"You do? Really?"

Scott mistook my excitement for surprise. "Yeah," he smiled. "Why so surprised? Don't you think I got it in me?"

"Oh, sure," I apologized. "It's just that . . ." Now it was my turn to be shy.

"Come on," Scott urged. "I can take it."

"No it's not that." I felt my face growing red. "It's just that I like to write plays. Short ones," I added.

Scott's eyes widened. "Really? That's great! Maybe I can read them sometime."

"Well," I blushed. I can't remember ever having blushed so much. "I'm not sure they're any good."

"Aw come on," Scott smiled. "In ten years we'll both have our names in lights." Scott squinted and pointed to the menu over the counter. "Scott Miles in a new play by Sandi Peters," he pretended to read.

We both laughed. Then Scott clinked my glass with his. "To Broadway."

I'd only had a cherry coke. But I felt like I'd been downing double martinis. By the time I got home my head was spinning. I liked Scott. Really.

Saturday finally came. I woke up at six A.M. I was too excited to sleep. What was I going to do with myself, I wondered, as I put on my jeans. It was too early to call anyone.

I tiptoed down to the kitchen. I pulled out Mom's recipe book. Banana bread and chocolate chip cookies. Coming up.

By the time Mom came downstairs the bread was in the oven, and I was whipping up batter for the cookies.

"My, something smells good," Mom said, walking in. Then she stopped and surveyed my creative cooking. Dirty pots and pans were all over the place. "Just make sure you do a good clean-up. The Framptons are coming to dinner tonight."

Cookie batter almost splattered to my feet. "But Mom, I'm going to a party. That's why I'm baking."

Mom frowned. "Whose party?"

"Toni Diamond. Remember you told me you met her mother in the supermarket."

"Oh yes," Mom remembered. "Nice woman." Mom looked disturbed. Then she brightened. I braced myself. Her ideas usually meant trouble.

"Well you can take Martha with you," she said. "One person more or less wouldn't hurt anybody."

"But Mom . . ." I was about to tell her that it was couples, but I stopped. They'd insist on Scott picking me up at the house and then quiz him for hours. Besides, I didn't even know his phone number. ". . . she might not like it."

Mom frowned again. "Why not? What are you going to *do* there?"

I knew I was stuck. If I tried too hard to convince Mom, she wouldn't let me go at all.

"I just can't call this dinner off," Mom said, during my silence. "It's important for your father. And I'm sure Martha would love to go."

As I watched Mom walk away, tears filled my eyes. Sure, Martha would just love it. Being at a party with a bunch of kids she hardly knew. Being the only one without a date. Sure, I thought. She'll be doing somersaults.

I put my mixing bowl down. But Martha's happiness wasn't my biggest worry. Kathy said that Toni didn't like her. What if Toni wouldn't let her come?

But I knew I had to try. I knew my parents. It was take Martha, or no party. Period.

I decided to call Kathy. Maybe she could help.

"What a bummer," Kathy said after I'd told her.

"But Martha's really okay," I insisted. "She wouldn't ruin anyone's fun."

At first Kathy didn't answer. "Listen," she finally said. "I'll call Toni. Stay by the phone. I'll call you right back."

After what seemed like ten years the phone rang.

"She can come," Kathy told me. "Toni's even inviting an extra guy."

I was almost too excited to speak. "Who?" I finally managed to ask.

"I don't know," she said. "But I told her to invite someone nice."

One down and one to go. I still had to call Martha.

"I don't think Toni likes me," she said after I'd invited her.

"Why not?"

"She once tried to copy my test. I wouldn't let her."

So that was it. My mind raced. I had to make her say yes.

"Of course she does," I insisted. I decided to tell a little lie. It wouldn't hurt anyone. And it would make Martha feel better. "In fact," I said, "when I told her we were friends, she asked me to bring you along."

By the time I put down the receiver I felt like I'd been through a war. But at least I'd come out on the winning side.

The Framptons arrived about twenty minutes late. I was more than ready. I should have been. I spent practically the whole day dressing.

"Come on up," I yelled to Martha.

For a moment I thought she was someone else. Martha looked so different. She was wearing a beautiful skirt of soft pastels and her hair had a nice wave. She was wearing lipstick too, and there was color in her face.

"You look great," I told her.

"You too," she said.

You'd think Martha and I were leaving the country, our parents gave us so many instructions. But finally we were out.

"How many kids did Toni invite?" Martha asked as we walked along.

I was going to tell Martha about being paired off, but I decided against it. I didn't want her to back down now. "Not too many," I said.

But I wondered who Toni did invite for her. She looked so happy. I really hoped it would be someone nice.

You could hear music even before we got to the house. Martha slowed down. I felt like running. "Don't be afraid," I told her. "It's only a party." Sure.

Toni's door was open, so we just walked in.

"Everyone's downstairs," Mrs. Diamond smiled at us.

I was almost glad Martha was with me. I didn't feel like making my grand entrance alone.

At first I hardly recognized anything in the soft light. The basement looked so different. Silver streamers twisted from the ceiling. Black balloons bobbled everywhere. It looked like some crazy nightclub out of the 1930s. Very art deco.

"The place looks great," Martha said as I put my banana bread and cookies on the refreshment table. "But everyone looks paired off."

I nodded, but I was too busy surveying the dancing couples to answer. I didn't see Scott anywhere.

"Who's that sitting in the corner?" Martha asked. "Isn't that Johnny Wimple?"

I looked. Light seemed to bounce off his black, greasy hair. It was definitely Johnny. Oh no, I thought. How could Toni do such a rotten thing?

But then I stopped thinking. I heard a familiar voice.

"Excuse me, does anyone have this dance?"

It was Scott. My heart did something funny. He came over.

"Go ahead," Martha said after they'd met. "I'll be okay."

But suddenly we had company.

"You Martha?" Johnny Wimple asked.

She nodded.

"I'm Johnny Wimple."

We all stared at him. Johnny slouched into his shoes. "Ummm . . . how about some punch?" He chuckled. "The drinking kind. I don't dance like that." He motioned to some kids doing the Hustle.

"Neither do I," Martha said stiffly. Then she looked at me. It was a look I would have preferred not to see. Her eyes watered. Like a hurt puppy. Then she turned to Johnny. "But punch would be nice."

As they walked away, I saw Toni. She was watching while she laughed and whispered something to Marlene.

For a moment I wanted to rush over and wring her lousy neck. But Scott was talking to me.

"Hey. My legs are falling asleep."

I looked into Scott's smiling eyes. There was nothing I could do about Martha now, I thought. She was a big girl. She'd have to take care of herself.

"Just keep them off my toes," I answered.

I laughed, but somehow it didn't sound quite right.

Scott was a great dancer. Was I glad that Ann taught me the Hustle.

"Hi, Sandi," she called as we twirled by her and her date, Dan Williams.

"Hi," I waved back. Ann really looked beautiful. I hoped that Scott wouldn't notice too much.

"He's very cute," she mouthed the words behind Scott's back.

"I know," I laughed back. Not too cute, I hoped.

We twirled by Susan and Tommy McAllister. She invited him after all! Good work!

I waved to Susan, but she didn't see. She was lost in Tommy.

"You're a pretty good dancer," Scott said when the music stopped.

"Thank you," I blushed.

He squeezed my arm. "And," he added in a dashing gentleman's voice, "did I tell you that you look lovely tonight."

I was glad he said it that way. So he wouldn't embarrass me.

"So glad you think so," I answered in a high society lady's voice. "This gown cost a fortune."

We both laughed. I was wearing a loose blouse and skirt.

We danced several more fast numbers. Then a slow dance came on. Suddenly, everyone developed a terrific thirst.

"Don't you work at the hardware store?" Tommy McAllister asked Scott as we crowded around the punch.

Soon Tommy and Kathy's boyfriend were talking to Scott, so I joined Susan and Kathy.

"Neat blouse," Susan complimented me.

We all admired each other's clothes. And dates. Then Susan pointed to the corner.

"Isn't that Martha Frampton with Johnny Wimple?" she asked.

Kathy nodded. "Toni fixed them up."

I looked over at Martha. Johnny was talking and Martha was nodding her head. Her face looked serious.

"Looks like he's bending her ear off," Susan giggled.

Suddenly, I felt my face grow red. "Did you know Toni was inviting Johnny?" I asked Kathy.

Kathy shrugged. "Toni's no magician. Not everyone's dying to go out with Martha."

I nodded. But I wondered if Kathy really believed that.

Then a fast dance came on.

"Come on everybody," someone yelled. "Let's line up."

This was a dance I knew from Wisconsin. Everyone formed lines. We all scrambled onto the floor. Only Tommy McAllister added a new variation.

"Do the ape," he yelled. As he danced, he hunched his back.

The guys joined right in. We females weren't crazy about clumping around like clumsy goons. But then someone yelled "Do the swan" and we were a symphony of arms. Mostly dying, of course.

It wasn't until someone yelled "drunken fish" and everyone started staggering around that I noticed Martha again. This time she was laughing. But not at Johnny Wimple's great wit. Toni's date, Rob London, was sitting beside her. And the two of them were cracking up.

Good, I thought.

Then someone changed the record. The Beatles came on.

Kathy's date grabbed my hand. "My turn," he smiled.

We didn't do the Hustle. We danced apart. Scott and Kathy joined. Then another couple came out on the floor. Martha and Rob London!

Dancing alone gave me a chance to look around. I watched Johnny Wimple cross the floor and ask Toni to dance.

Toni stared right past him. At Martha and Rob. She looked angry. Then she started to dance with Johnny.

The record changed again. A slow dance came on. This time everyone didn't rush off the floor. We changed partners. I was back with Scott.

Scott put his arms around me. It felt very nice. "Having a good time?" he asked.

I smiled back. I really was.

As we danced, I closed my eyes.

"Excuse me," someone bumped into us. It was Martha and Rob London. They were still together. Toni must be having a cow, I thought happily.

After the dance I excused myself. I wanted to fix my hair. It was beginning to droop.

When I came back down, everyone was crowded around the refreshment table. Mostly eating and talking. I started walking toward Scott, when it happened.

Toni was talking to Marlene. Martha was standing close by. I watched Toni look at Martha. I watched her take aim. Then, she spilled her punch. All over Martha's skirt.

"Oh," Martha cried.

"I'm so sorry," Toni apologized. But I knew that wasn't true. I saw her do it!

The punch was very red. Martha's skirt was very light. "Looks like blood," Johnny Wimple said.

A few kids laughed. Martha ran from the room. "Wait," I yelled. But Martha didn't stop.

"God, she's sensitive," Toni was saying. "Honestly. I didn't see her standing there."

I stared at Toni. Blood rushed to my face. I couldn't let her get away with it. Not again.

"That's not true," I cried. "You did it on purpose. I saw you."

Everyone got very quiet. Toni looked like she'd been slapped. "Are you crazy?" she spat. "She bumped into my arm." She turned to Marlene. "Right?"

Marlene nodded. Of course.

"Listen," Tommy McAllister said. "There's no reason to fight. It was an accident, that's all."

I heard someone shouting. Myself. "It was not an accident. It was a dirty trick."

Then I ran out. I had to find Martha.

Martha was halfway down the block. Crying.

"Go away," she said.

"Martha. Please. Let me explain."

I forced Martha to listen. I told her everything. How I didn't know about Johnny Wimple.

Martha stopped crying. "I knew Toni didn't like me," she sniffed.

"Who cares?" I said. That was funny. I really meant it.

"But I've caused you so much trouble," Martha said. "I feel like such an idiot."

I smiled. "Me? You're the one with a ruined dress."

Martha smiled back. "I can afford to buy a new one."

We laughed. Then we started walking. I thought about everyone back at the party. And I thought about Scott. I couldn't just leave him. Maybe he thought I was crazy.

Then I heard a voice.

"Wait up."

My heart jumped. It was Scott. On his bicycle. "I'm sorry about your dress," he said to Martha.

"That's okay."

"Quite a commotion back there." He paused. "But that's still no reason to let me ride home alone." He looked around, pretending to be frightened. "It's scary around here."

We all laughed. The street was suburban and well-lit.

"What kind of commotion?" I asked. I had to know.

"Oh," he raised his eyes, like it was all ridiculous. "Toni called you a liar, I think. But Ann stuck up for you. She called Toni a witch, and left."

Goose pimples blossomed on my skin. Ann. She was a friend.

"What about Kathy?" I asked.

Scott laughed. "What do I look like? A newspaper?"

Scott walked his bicycle alongside of us. What now, I wondered.

"Maybe we can all go out sometime," Scott said. He looked at Martha. "I have a friend."

Martha raised her hand in protest. "No more blind dates," she laughed.

Scott laughed. So did I. For a different reason. Scott wanted to see me again!

"Well, all right," Scott smiled. "With whomever you like."

Soon we were at my house.

"Goodnight," Scott smiled. "I'll call you soon. Okay?"

Okay? Of course! "Sure."

We watched Scott ride off. Then we heard our parents inside.

"Sandi, is that you?" Mom called.

"I guess we'd better go in," Martha said.

I thought about my parents. They would be glad I came home with Martha. That was them all over. Doing the right things for the wrong reasons. Then I thought about myself. I felt kind of proud. Maybe I lost a crowd. But I gained a friend. Three of them. Maybe more.

"Let's go," I smiled. "I'll let you borrow something."

About the Author

The author of several books for young readers, Ellen Rabinowich has also acted professionally and produced a dramatic film feature. Her experience in the theater and as an educational script writer were useful in working on the current novella, *Toni's Crowd*. Ms. Rabinowich lives and works in New York City. She is also the author of *Kangaroos, Koalas, and Other Maruspials* in the Franklin Watts First Book series.

About
the Photographer

G. Richardson Cook has worked as a music producer, film director, and screenwriter. He was born on Nantucket Island and lives in New York City.

FIC
RAB   Rabinowich, Ellen

              Toni's crowd

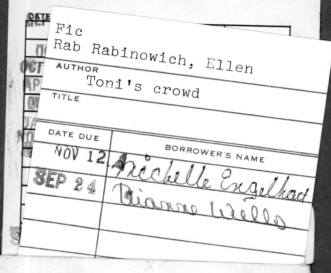

Fic
Rab Rabinowich, Ellen
AUTHOR
       Toni's crowd
TITLE

DATE DUE	BORROWER'S NAME
NOV 12	Michelle Engelhard
SEP 24	Dianne Wells